EXTRA YARN

BY
MAC BARNETT

ILLUSTRATED BY
JON KLASSEN

First published in Great Britain 2013 by Walker Books Ltd
87 Vauxhall Walk, London SE11 5HJ

This edition published 2014

First published in the United States 2012 by Balzer + Bray. Published by arrangement
with HarperCollins Children's Books, a division of HarperCollins, Inc.

2 4 6 8 10 9 7 5 3 1

Text © 2012 Mac Barnett
Illustrations © 2012 Jon Klassen

The right of Mac Barnett and Jon Klassen to be identified as
author and illustrator respectively of this work has been asserted by them
in accordance with the Copyright, Designs and Patents Act 1988

This book has been typeset in Cloister

Printed in China

British Library Cataloguing in Publication Data:
a catalogue record for this book is available from the British Library

ISBN 978-1-4063-5248-1

www.walker.co.uk

For Steven Malk
M.B.

For Mom
J.K.

On a cold afternoon, in a cold little town,
where everywhere you looked was either the white of snow
or the black of soot from chimneys,
Annabelle found a box filled with yarn of every colour.

So she went home and
knitted herself a jumper.

And when Annabelle
was done, she had
some extra yarn.

So she knitted a jumper for Mars, too.

But there was still extra yarn.

And when Annabelle and Mars went
for a walk, Luke pointed and laughed
and said, "You two look ridiculous."

"You're just jealous,"
said Annabelle.

"No, I'm not," said Luke.

But it turned out he was.

And even after she'd made a jumper for Luke
and his dog, and for herself and for Mars,
she still had extra yarn.

At school, Annabelle's classmates could
not stop talking about her jumper.

"Quiet!" shouted Mr Norman.

"Quiet, everyone! Annabelle, that jumper of yours is a terrible distraction. I cannot teach with everyone turning around to look at you!"

"Then I'll knit one for everyone," Annabelle said, "so they won't have to turn around."

"Impossible!" said Mr Norman. "You can't."

But it turned out she could. And she did.

Even for Mr Norman.

And when she was done, Annabelle still had extra yarn.

So she knitted jumpers for her mum and dad.

And for Mr Pendleton

and Mrs Pendleton.

And for Dr Palmer.

And for little Louis.

She made jumpers for everyone, except
Mr Crabtree, who never wore jumpers or
even trousers, and who would stand in
his shorts with the snow up to his knees.
"No jumper for me, thanks," said Mr Crabtree.

So she made Mr Crabtree a hat.
And even then Annabelle still
had extra yarn.

She made jumpers for all the dogs,

and all the cats,

and for other animals, too.

Soon, people thought, soon Annabelle will run out of yarn.

But it turned out she didn't.

So Annabelle made jumpers for things
that didn't even wear jumpers.

Things began to change
in that little town.

News spread of this remarkable girl who never ran out of yarn.
And people came to visit from around the world, to see all the jumpers
and to shake Annabelle's hand.

One day an archduke, who was very fond of clothes,
sailed across the sea and demanded to see Annabelle.

"Little girl," said the archduke, "I would like to buy that miraculous box of yarn. And I am willing to offer you one million pounds."

"No, thank you," said Annabelle, who was knitting a jumper for a pickup truck.

The archduke's moustache twitched.
"Two million," he said.

Annabelle shook her head.
"No thanks."

"Ten million!" shouted the
archduke. "Take it or leave it!"

"Leave it," said Annabelle.
"I won't sell the yarn."

And she didn't.

So that night the archduke hired three robbers
to break into Annabelle's house,

and they stole the box

and took it to the archduke,
who set off across the snow,
and sailed over the sea,

back to his castle.

The archduke put on his favourite song
and sat in his best chair.
Then he took out the box,
and he lifted its lid, and he looked inside.

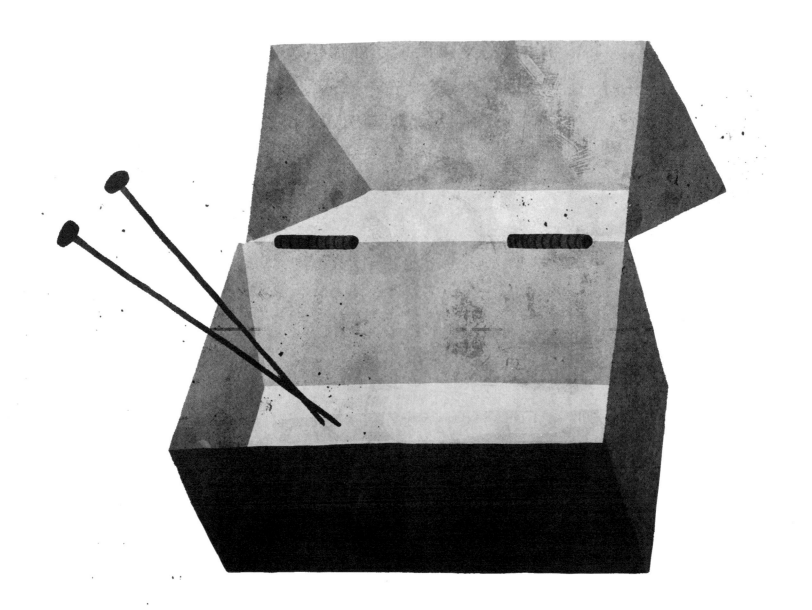

His moustache quivered.

It shivered.

It trembled.

The archduke hurled the box
out the window and shouted,
"Little girl, I curse you with
my family's curse!
You will never be happy again!"

But

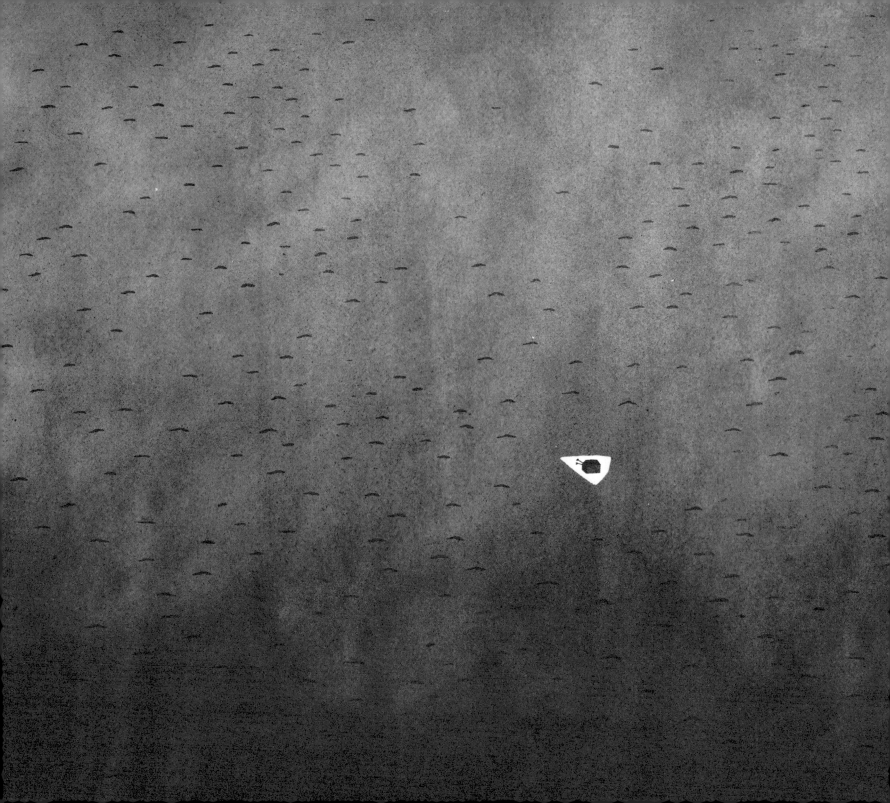

it turned out she was.

MAC BARNETT is the author of several picture books, including *Chloe and the Lion* and *Guess Again!* He lives in the USA, in Berkeley, California.

JON KLASSEN won the prestigious 2010 Canadian Governor General's Award for children's literature (illustration). The author-illustrator of the multiple-award-winning *I Want My Hat Back* and the 2013 Caldecott Medal-winning *This Is Not My Hat*, he was named a 2013 Caldecott Honor recipient for his illustrations for *Extra Yarn*. Originally from Niagara Falls, Canada, Jon now lives in the USA, in Los Angeles.